Jan Pieńkowski

Bel and Bub

and the Bad Snowball

DK

A Dorling Kindersley Book

It was winter.
Bel was playing house.

Bub was bored.

Suddenly a snowball whizzed through the window.

It hit Bel's
house like an avalanche.

Bel was very angry.

I'm going out with Meph

It was Meph. He had
come to play with Bub.

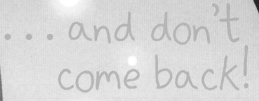

...and don't come back!

Bel was left behind.

Bub and Meph raced
off into the snow.

They made a snow angel.

They gave it a grumpy face
and twigs for wings.

Tee hee,
it's Bel !

They made a halo out
of Meph's scarf.

Now it looked just like
Bel in a bad mood.

Bel came
out to look at their snow angel.